This Little Tiger book belongs to:

_____

_____

_____

_____

For Sarah and Benjamin
J.W.

For George
T.W.

LITTLE TIGER PRESS
An imprint of Magi Publications
1 The Coda Centre, 189 Munster Road, London SW6 6AW, UK
www.littletigerpress.com
First published in Great Britain 1999
by Little Tiger Press, London
This edition published 2008
Text copyright © Judy West 1999
Illustrations copyright © Tim Warnes 1999
Judy West and Tim Warnes have asserted their rights
to be identified as the author and illustrator of this work
under the Copyright, Designs and Patents Act, 1988
All rights reserved • ISBN 978-1-84506-510-2
Printed in China
2 4 6 8 10 9 7 5 3 1

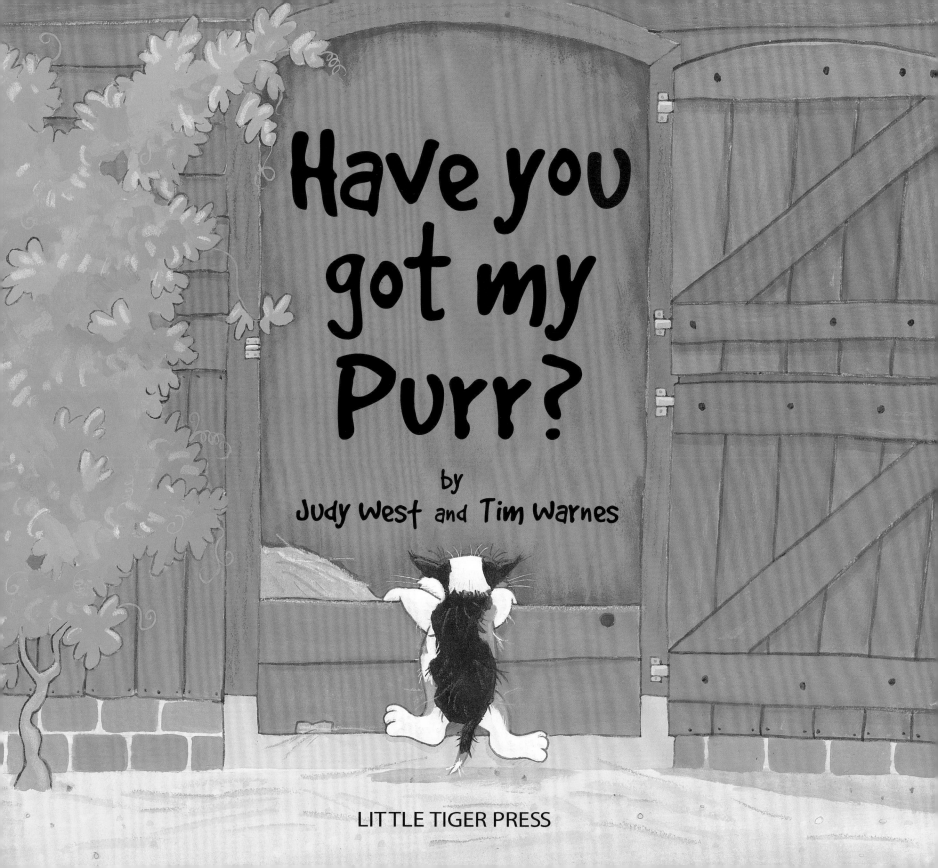

Have you got my Purr?

by
Judy West and Tim Warnes

LITTLE TIGER PRESS

Kitten was sad. She could mew, she could hiss, and she could yowl, but she couldn't make the noise she liked the best—she couldn't purr.

"Mother," she said, "I think I've lost my purr."

"Little one," her mother replied, "you will find your purr. Just wait and see."

Wait? The determined kitten set out in search
of her purr. She decided that Dog might have it.
"Dog," Kitten asked, "have you got my purr?"
She climbed onto his belly to listen closely
to his answer.

"Woof woof," said the startled dog. "I have a woof, not a purr. Why don't you ask Cow? She may have it."

So Kitten went off to do just that.
She found a perch next to the
paddock and very near Cow's head.
"Cow," Kitten said, looking her right
in the eye, "have you got my purr?
Dog says you might."

MOO

MOO

"Moo moo," said Cow quickly. "I have my moo, but no purr. Why not ask Pig?"

Kitten slid slowly down the tree and scampered over to the pigpen and up the fence.

"Pig! Have you got my purr?" she called over the snuffling of the piglets.

OINK OINK OINK OINK

"Oink oink," said Pig. "I am sorry, dear.
I have only my oink, no purr.
Why don't you ask the Ducks?
They are a noisy family."

So Kitten followed the sounds of splashing and found the Ducks enjoying their day-long bath.

"Ducks, I've asked Dog and Cow and Pig, but they don't seem to have it. Have *you* got my purr?"

QUACK

QUACK

"Quack quack," said the Ducks. "Does that sound like a purr? We quack."

One duck offered kindly, "Why not ask Mouse?"

This would be tricky, but Kitten really wanted her purr back. She scooted over to the mouse hole, got down on her belly, and wiggled through.

"Don't be afraid, Mouse," said Kitten very quietly. "You see, I am searching for something. Have you got my purr?"

"Squeak squeak," said Mouse nervously. "I have my squeak, Kitten, but I do not have your purr. Have you asked squeak— I mean, Sheep?"

SQUEAK SQUEAK

A little discouraged and very tired, Kitten hung her head and wandered over to the field. "Sheep," she sighed, "I have lost my purr. Mouse says you might have it. Have you got my purr?"

"Baa baa," said Sheep. "I haven't got your purr, little one. My old baa is all I have. Why not ask Owl?"

So Kitten stumbled sleepily over to Owl's tree and said, "Owl, I have searched all day. I'm so tired. Have you got my purr?"

"Hoot hoot," Owl said. "Silly kitten, I have a hoot, not a purr. Why don't you go back to your mother? I'm sure you'll find your purr there."

Kitten couldn't believe it. Has Mother had my purr all along? she wondered.

She rushed back to the barn to call out her question one last time. "Mother, have you got my purr?"

"Oh, sweet thing," said her mother tenderly, "no one can take your purr. It's inside you. You hear it when you're happy. Come here and listen."

So Kitten snuggled next to
her mother, and suddenly . . .

. . . there it was!
The dog did not woof.
The cow did not moo.
The pig did not oink.
The ducks did not quack.
The mouse did not squeak.
The sheep did not baa.
The owl did not hoot.

They all watched from the
door and listened silently to
the most perfect purr they
had ever heard.

PURR PURR

fantastic reads from Little Tiger Press

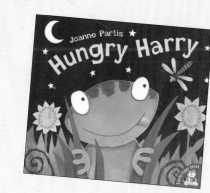

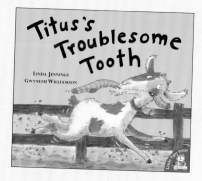

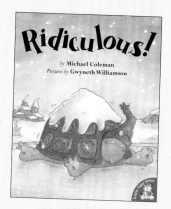

For information regarding any of the above titles
or for our catalogue, please contact us:
Little Tiger Press, 1 The Coda Centre,
189 Munster Road, London SW6 6AW, UK
Tel: +44 (0)20 7385 6333 Fax: +44 (0)20 7385 7333
E-mail: info@littletiger.co.uk
www.littletigerpress.com

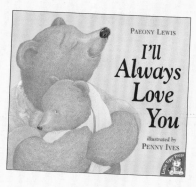